This book belongs to

....

make believe ideas ltd

The Wilderness, Berkhamsted, Hertfordshire, HP4 2AZ, UK.
501 Nelson Place, P.O. Box 141000, Nashville, TN 37214-1000, USA.

www.makebelieveideas.com

Written by Nick Page.
Illustrated by Clare Fennell.

Oh, no, Mr. Snowman!

Clare Fennell • Nick Page

make believe ideas

"Come on! Let's build a snowman!"

Katy said to me.

So we did.

We built a snowman, Katy and me,

and we called him "Mr. Snowman."

We played with Mr. Snowman all afternoon, Katy and me,
and when it got cold, Mom called us in to eat.

We ate our food, Katy and me.
But something was wrong.

The fish sticks were still frozen,
    the beans were crunchy with frost,
and our hot chocolate was **really cold.**

Then we saw him . . .
Can you see him?

* FROSTY *

- jello
- yule log
- ice cream
- pudding

Oh, no, Mr. Snowman! You CAN'T come in here!

We played with Mr. Snowman the next day, Katy and me,
and when it got late, Mom called us in for story time.

But something was wrong.

My book had frozen shut,
   the sofa was covered in snow,
and the room was **really,**
      really cold.

Then we saw him . . .
   Can you see him?

Oh, no, Mr. Snowman! You CAN'T come in here!

Cats are allowed indoors, snowmen aren't.

We played with Mr. Snowman the next day, Katy and me,
and when we got tired, Mom called us in to have our bath.
But something was wrong.

Our towels were as hard as wood,
there were icebergs in the bathtub,
and the water was **really, really,
really cold**.

Then we saw him . . .
Can you see him?

Oh, no, Mr. Snowman! You CAN'T come in here!

And STAY OUT!

We played with Mr. Snowman the next day, Katy and me,
and when it got dark, Mom called us in and put us to bed.

But something was wrong.

My pillow was like a lump of ice,
Katie's teddy bear was frozen solid,
and we were **really, really,**
really cold.

Then we saw him . . .
Can you see him?

Oh, no, Mr. Snowman! You CAN'T come in here!

say "No" to snowmen!

The next day... it was Christmas Eve!

All of our relatives came to visit.

But something was wrong.

The ice cream was runny,
the jello wasn't set,
and everything was **really, really,**
really hot!

The fridge was broken!

Then there was a
knock at the door.

Knock!
Knock!

Who could it be?

Oh, yes, Mr. Snowman. You CAN come in here!

Mr. Snowman iced all the ice creams
and set all the jello.
Mr. Snowman made
everything snowy!

Everyone was **really happy** that Mr. Snowman had come indoors.

Ha, ha!

To Katie and Me

You can't catch me!

Well . . . almost everyone.